INDISTINCT
CONVERSATIONS

AUSTIN JAMES

Indistinct Conversations is dedicated to my mother. She should be appalled by the disgusting shit that I write but is blinded by love for her only son.

Runners up for dedication include Garrett Cook, Richard Thomas, and S.C. Burke. Many great writers/teachers have taught me so much about craft and storytelling, but without the three of you I'd never be able to get the word chaos out onto the page in a readable fashion.

CONTENTS

Benchwarmer

The garden bench near the front door, with its smooth, narrow cedar slats and the decorative cast iron frame, that you painted Fern Green and then, years later, Puritan Blue (but is now a distinguished greying wood that sheds faded paint shavings) our initials and the date we were wed carved into the backrest where no one else can see, a hidden keepsake for just the two of us, where I held you tight after the first miscarriage, the bench offering more comfort than a pew down at Saint John's ever could—but also where we watched our daughter Maggie teeter without training wheels, stopping after a few lines in the sidewalk's concrete to make sure we'd seen her, nearly as proud of herself as we are of her; the very bench I sat chain-smoking (numbing our debt with tequila) for hours before admitting I'd lost my job, where I rested my fatigue, hiding my hunger because it was more important for you two to eat when we couldn't afford more, where Maggie wept the first time her date never showed, and I felt like hunting the punk down to threaten his life, but you talked me into realizing I knew better; the bench I sat every night that year you took Maggie and moved into that damn apartment across town, trying not to let myself get drunk, hoping every passing car was you coming home, where I listened to the breeze push curled, dead leaves across the driveway—scraping like hollowed chalk—the night my dad died, where Maggie had her first kiss even though she didn't know you saw from inside the house, where I ended up chiseling fossilized clumps of chewing gum from the underbelly, you forbidding me from being a jerk about it, where I slept that summer night long ago after we fought over something insignificant, eventually seeking chiropractic realignment for my spine because I was too stubborn to go back inside; the bench where we'd prop up our jack-olanterns (remember that year Maggie's ex-boyfriend got his revenge my thrashing our pumpkins in the street?), where I staggered and fell onto when I had my heart attack, leading to a hospital stay that had to be more frightening for you than it was for me, where we caught Maggie smoking pot in the dark and laughed about it later, teasing her for not sharing, where the occasional springtime songbird would perch and prune its feathers; the bench where we sat and delayed our tears while watching her pull away in her secondhand Subaru, university bound, this nest in her rearview mirror, where we've sat countless times and watched the sun come up over the jagged jawline of the Wasatch mountains, sipping hot coffee (inkwell black for me, two sugars and a dab of creamer for you) sometimes with favored liquor on special occasions; the garden bench that's forlorn and barren since you passed on… has grown rickety, and I've become cold once again, needing something to burn to keep from freezing before morning.

Innards

(*A*nd *then there were two)*
(me and this fucken guy…)

(Truck leans back into his chair, face indifferent, eyes squinty, bloodshot)

(tells me):

Had this collie when I was a lad. Fooken thing kept dig'n holes all over the place. I loved that dog—didn't care that it fooked up the yard. Me pa, though, he hated the thing. Hated all the holes it dug.

(he leans forward again, elbows on table, eyes attempting intensity)

Every time Pa'd come home to find a new hole, he'd act all not-pissed-off and call the mutt: 'come eer'. And the damn dog'd run right over to him, all dumb 'n happy, every time. And me pa? Well he'd grab it by the collar and beat the shite outta it—like, beat it until actual shite drip'd straight outta its fooken arse. Heard the whimpers in me dreams for years.

(his right eye behaves slightly lopsided compared to the left)

Yessir, Pa'd hit that mutt 'till his fists got tired. Then he'd fill the hole up with water and shove its snout right down in it. Hold its face underwater there until it stopped squirm'n, then he'd make me count to three—all bawl'n and snotty-nosed, just a kid mind ye. On me count of three, he'd yank its nose back out of the water, pet'n it and speak'n all soft-like. After it'd calm down he'd go back to punch'n the fooker a few more times and shove its head back in the water.

(leans back again, grinning eyes of a man who believes he's won)

Pa thought the dog'd learn to quit dig'n the fooken holes,

ye see? But it never did. He ended up drown'n that ole mutt when I was twelve or thirteen, I reckon.

(I respond):

Soooo your daddy waterboarded your puppy? I guess that's how I'm supposed to know you're a tough motherfucker, huh?

(he swallows his smile)

Me pa was a failure. And ye know I'm a tough motherfooker cuz I've got this…

(nods towards the envelope on the table between us)

His eyes are brown coffee but weakening. We sit at a table beneath tavern floorboards (afterhours), the only ones still competing for undisputed rights to his envelope's contents. We twitch and shift and stare. Watching each other's pupils shrink and swell in the timid basement lighting. The others— the losers—stand around. Whispering. Waiting.

(my turn):

Alright, I've got one. So there I was, in the middle of the ocean…

Like, ye was on a fish'n boat?

Nope, just me and my personal floatation device. Anyways, it'd been several days and I was plenty wave-sick…

(his eyes stink of doubt)

What? Wait. How the fook did ye get out into the sea with just'a life vest?

From the plane crash.

Plane crash? What the fook, man?

Look, I listened to your weepy little dog story—which

7

was as boring as fuck, by the way—without a single complaint. You gonna keep interrupting and shit, or can I just tell my fucken story, man? Please!

(eyes widen in brevity...stoic facial expression swiftly regained)

(now he's wondering if anyone noticed his lapse in poise)

(nods for me to continue)

So...there I was, floating on my seat cushion in the middle of the ocean. Hadn't seen a fucken thing. No boat on the horizon, no exotic deserted island, not a fucken thing. Man, I'd have given anything to hallucinate a cheese burger or a hot dog like in those old timey cartoons, you know? Just to have something else to do out there, other than sauté in the sun that is. Know what I'm saying?

(eyes sprout a dash of boredom)

Now this is important, man. Just so you know what kind of shape I was in. Saturated with salt and seawater. Fuck, I think I had even lost a shoe at some point—could've been in the crash? Anyways, after enough days to lose count, what do you think I ran into? A motherfucking shark. Right? No shit, a goddamn shark. Just like in the movies. One of those ones with the wide faces. What are they called—hammerheaders? Anyways...

(irises quiver and eyebrows tilt)

...this fucken shark circles for what must've been hours. Weighing the pros and cons of eating a sickly thing like me. As it spirals in closer and closer, I dig into my pockets for some sort of weapon. I mean, not like I had a pocket knife or anything (what with being on the plane and all) but car keys maybe? But of course not. Just my credit card—not even my wallet, just the damn card. Anyways, I figured I'd be too weak to fight the fucken thing off, you know? But when it finally gets close enough to smell (sharks smell like seltzer water and dry rot tires, by the way), a strong dose of adrenaline hits the veins like nitroglycerin. Ever felt that? A burst of primal adrenaline so pure you can sense each individual sodium molecule inside every single drop of water in the never-ending ocean around you?

(eyes flicker pseudo-acknowledgement)

So, let me get this right. Ye were fooken stranded at sea, attacked by a fooken shark and yet, here ye are, in the flesh, today?

Right? And here's where it gets really wild: the shark comes in for the kill shot, right? Jagged-ass teeth, all scary and shit. I kick and scream and hoot and holler—pretty standard reaction for someone about to be eaten by a shark, yeah? I lash out at it with my credit card, trying to gouge out an eye or something. At least make my death a bit more heroic. Must've surprised the shark, cuz it slowed its attack some. Anyways, I hack at the eyes, but as the fucken thing splashes around, the card slips against its slickery skin and swipes through one it's gills. And the damn thing gets skittish. It just fucks off. Just leaves, swimming away all slow and limpy. Just straight up decided not to eat me. The fuck, right?

(eyes in various states of disbelief)

Ye mean to tell me…that ye defeated this shark by pay'n it off with your fooken credit card?!

Well, not exactly. Turns out, there's a hidden fee on most cards—you know, an extra percentage added in here and there—that pays for shark repellant. Something about the magnetic strip reminding them of their mothers, making them all nostalgic and gloomy and shit. Says right there in the fine print when you sign up. Heh, who knew? Hell, yours might have the same perk—you oughta look into it.

(silent confusion)

Bwahahahahahahahaha! Ye've got some brain twaddle, do ye? Coming in eer with a story like that. Ye caint really expect me to believe that shite. Ha!

Not really. But you blinked just now. I win.

(the small crowd agrees)

(gutwrench heaves his eyes from Glee to Denial to Anger)

(and then there was one)

Ye won't get away with this ye sneaky fooker! Ye'll see! Ye ain't seen the last 'o Truck motherfooken Anderson!

(he fucks off back upstairs to break into the liquor cabinet while I slide my envelope into a coat pocket)

(now the power is mine)

Rousting

lazy meteor spray
of hot cigarette ash from
the balcony/upstairs
neighbor is already awake
although it's too early
for foot-traffic.
cozy sheet of dew drapes
the lawn, the shrubbery,
the windshields of sleepy cars
(crowded together like cattle).
coffee: speechless black
with two ice cubes because
it's best at room temperature.
used to be, I'd have smoked a few
cigarettes by now. some mornings
are lonely empty
without them.

Recovery

Monica doesn't know the old me, before sobriety, but tearing apart her Kate Spade purse gives her a glimpse. I'm home late from work again and the kids are already in bed. And I forgot that this morning was our daughter's kindergarten recital. Monica doesn't mind spending the paychecks that late nights bring home—money that paid for her acrylic nails and the balayage highlights in her auburn hair. It's our first big fight as a married couple. She locks herself in our bedroom while I fall asleep on the couch, envious of emotionless men who can abandon their families.

Stringy red skin-blots appear on Junior's abdomen overnight, looking especially angry on his naturally pale skin. I suggest that our son may have a mild pox but Monica isn't in the mood. The closest pediatrician open on Saturdays is down in Dothan. Even though Junior is our second child, we decide to make the forty-five-minute drive instead of waiting until Monday. While driving I try to hold her hand, which jukes away to change the radio station. I can't hear anything over her thunderous silence. We pass empty fields with round bales of cotton, taller than our minivan, that look like large rolls of medical gauze.

A brief chronology of influenza: an infected stranger sneezes near you, ejecting thousands of dormant virus particles into the air. It's already too late; you inhale the infestation. They hijack host cells to abuse and brutalize.

Molecular manslaughter.

The waiting room's crowded and it smells like Lysol wipes and cough drops. Domesticated ferns hang wilted and weepy from hooks in the ceiling and the walls are painted green like healing bruises. A skinny boy with curly hair, sucking and slobbering on a stick of red licorice, watches us rummage for open seats. He scratches his throat as if the inside of his skin itches.

Breeding viruses overpopulate and attack the cells inside your gullet, leaving what feels like broken glass shredding your vocal chords.

After a minute, I get used to the whiney tone of sick kids that fills the room. Junior doesn't want to sit in his split vinyl seat, and he smells like watered-down ammonia, so I hand Monica the baby wipes. She doesn't respond, but takes him into the bathroom to change his diaper. Our daughter Kayla sits on my lap playing vocabulary and arithmetic games on her Leapfrog learning tablet and I can smell her tear-free watermelon shampoo. I tell her I'm proud of her. She smiles with adoring green eyes like she's never heard me say this before, then snorts a braid of snot back up her nose. I follow up with a tissue from Monica's purse.

Cells lining your sinuses are massacred. Fluids erupt through your nasal caverns. Your nostrils spew mucous like ruptured dams.

A clearing on the navy blue hard wearing carpet is the only area that's not congested with sick people. It's cluttered with playthings, sticky from the occasional splatter of sanitizer. Returning in a dry diaper, Junior finds a faded red Matchbox racecar to push across the floor. I search for Monica's whitewater eyes but they don't want to be found. Kayla soon trades the Leapfrog for a Barbie doll that is dressed like a cheerleader and has ash brown hair like her. Other kids loiter in the area playing with the rest of the toys. A little girl with pig-tails befriends Kayla. They're about the same height, although she's not as good with her words as Kayla is. She giggles often and coughs too much.

Infection soaks into your respiratory system. You hack the shrapnel of viral warfare up out of your lungs. Phlegm cuts like barbed wire.

Junior watches the girls from his side of the rug. There's no toy in Pig-Tails' hands. A six-month stretch in daycare taught him about the dangers of a communal toy box.

In daycare, you have a choice: take, or be taken from.

Kayla's smart, yet naive to the cruelty of desperation. Junior wants to warn his sister but can't find the words. His fingers twitch while the racecar idles in his hand.

Pig-Tails watches Barbie.

She giggles and steps closer. Smiles.

Preschool vocabulary. Eyes on the doll again.

Pig-Tails seizes the doll's head and arms. Kayla yelps.

She grips the doll around the waist with both hands.

Little girl tug-of-war.

Screeching.

Junior's face clenches like a fist as he fast-balls the diecast car at Pig-Tails. It slaps into the side of her jawbone with a collision of shock and tears.

———

Monica takes Pig-Tails by the hand, fluttering eyes searching for the mother. The mom, a tall blonde with big teeth and a Crimson Tide tee-shirt, materializes to the sound of her daughter's whimper. Motherly instinct on autopilot.

"I keep telling her to play nice, bless her heart," Blonde Mom says, pulling Pig-Tails into a mother's healing embrace. "She'll be okay…just scared her more than anything. We're here because her arms and legs hurt all night, so she's already had plenty of Tylenol."

Your bloodstream becomes polluted. Viral insurgents rip through tissues and fibers. Your muscles smolder.

The two women keep talking because strangers are friends in the South; although I've learned to tell when Monica is just being polite. She's already said more to Blonde Mom than she has to me all morning, but at least she's laughing. Junior spots a three-wheeled firetruck to play with while Kayla straightens Barbie's cheer uniform.

I'm proud of Junior for defending his sister. Even if just toddler reaction, his fluid act of selflessness ricochets around my brain. Fighting for sobriety took an extreme amount of self-interest, putting *my* needs ahead of others for the first time in my life. Monica sees me watching her as I ponder this and smiles, calming the regret and worry that's been quietly boiling in my stomach. Have I traded addiction of booze for addiction of ego?

Could it be that my little boy is teaching *me* how to be a man?

The Everyday

Headlights bleed through
the night, black as
mechanic-shop coffee.

Headed south on Highway 93
towards the Nevada boarder.
Cigarette butt out the window

explodes like a firecracker
fizzling on the asphalt.
With the corporate

entourage and their
prostituted morals.

The "ifuckedsomeoneelse"s

and whiskey dick whiplash.
63 miles an hour behind,
dying the rearview mirror.

Violet Crime
Or Secondary colors

"What's the difference between a plummie and a speedbump? You slow down for the speedbump." Jimmie says, enjoying a smirk from his boss, Mr. McMillion, a man with skin as nectarine as his. They joke and laugh; reminisce.

Jimmie's greasy black hair hints gray at the temples; his tattoos stonewashed. A life of hard labor carved his body rock-solid as a tombstone. His lobster-tail chin stays mostly curled up against his neck nowadays.

"Anyway, Jimmie, I've summoned you to my office so we can have a talk," McMillion's slimy, dangly earthworm dundrearies droop from his jowls and squirm as he talks. He snags a filterless cigarette out of a squishy soft pack and lights it with a brass zippo engraved with dollar signs. "The world is changing. You've seen the purple propaganda—it's everywhere. I mean, there are equal rights protests in the capital for christsakes."

"Goddam grapers."

"Economy has changed, too. Things have gotten awfully political, old friend," he pauses. "There's no easy way to say this, so I'll just say it. Your job is being consolidated."

"*Consolidated*? The hell does that mean?!"

"This is a competitive market." When he speaks, his cigarette spews clumps of heavy ash all over his desk with each accentuating gesture. The earthworms growing from his fat cheeks stretch, trying to catch and eat them as they fall. "And I just can't compete paying orange man wages…it's why I've been hiring strictly purples the last couple years."

"This is bullshit, Bill!"

"Look, you've got a choice. You can either accept lower wages or look for work elsewhere."

"But I've been with this warehouse since I was a boy. Been a model employee."

"It's not personal, Jimmie, its business. Go home and think on it—I'll need your answer in the morning."

———

Lucas ties his hand-me-down work boots and watches his lavender wife make a bottle for their beautiful, purple baby boy.

"That's the last of the formula," she says. It's become a common saying in their studio apartment, overcrowded by just the three of them. Rumbling stomachs, rowdy neighbors, and avoiding the landlord are also common.

"We'll make due somehow," he says, standing and moving in to give her a goodbye kiss. She turns her face away.

"You always say that."

"And we always do. I've got to go to work."

"If you can call it that."

"What is that supposed to mean?"

"They barely pay you. You might as well be a slave."

Lucas whips his arms wide and raises his voice, "Yet we're better off than we were before I got this job, aren't we, Lidia?"

"You let them walk all over you."

"Look, I'm not exactly in a position to do anything else; a nightshift worker with less than a month's experience…"

"It's a good thing Junior is too young to know his father doesn't have the courage to demand a better wage."

Lucas scowls into her cantankerous eyes and blusters out of the apartment.

———

"Goddam purple-skinned scumbags, taking our jobs…it ain't right. These jobs are for good, hard-working orange folk." Jimmie and his friends loiter, like always, outside of Sal's, drinking beers and smoking cigarettes—their typical after-work hobby. They all have orange skin, one friend with automotive drive axles for arms; the back of another's head is a toilet paper dispenser, tissue crusty and gray with age.

Lucas walks to work at a pace faster than usual, angry, replaying his wife's ungrateful flareup. His body's not quite used to the new job at the warehouse, but he doesn't complain. After months without work, he finally has a job—and Lidia should be thankful for that. Bitch. Besides, as tall and slender as he is, he's always wanted a bit more muscle mass anyway.

"There's one of 'em now," Jimmie says, nodding down the sidewalk towards Lucas. "I'll bet that's one of the vermin that took an orange man's job at the warehouse…maybe not, they all look the same to me." His friends snicker.

Lucas sees them sitting at a table outside of the shithole bar. They're staring at him, glaring at him, talking shit: "Hey, plummie. Where you going?" Lucas ignores the racist jerkoffs.

Jimmie takes a sip of his beer and stands just in time to block the young purple man's path, belching beer and tooth decay into his face. "I asked you a question, graper."

Lucas goes to step around the large man, who moves in stride with him to impede his escape.

"What's the hurry? Late for a hot date or something? Maybe I should go with you, teach the bitch what a real man tastes like, not some earring-wearing punk like you. You can watch…I know you're into that kind of shit. Filthy fuckin' plummie."

Lucas's teeth grind, but thinking of his baby's innocent smile calms him. "No thanks, friend, my lady likes her grape juice just the way she gets it." The smartass in him always has the worst timing.

Jimmie's face reddens in the heat of embarrassment, shrinks into a scowl. No graper's gonna talk back to him, especially not in front of his friends. Not at Sal's. "The hell you say to me, boy?" he grunts, cracking his knuckles.

The punk doesn't respond, so Jimmie halfheartedly slaps him across the face. His pals burst with laughter as the purple's head whips to the side from the backhanded impact. "Whatchya gonna do about it, plummie?"

Lucas' face stings. He takes a deep breath and turns around as if to leave the way he came from, but suddenly spins to his right, thrusting the back of his fist into the prick's jaw. Spit and blood spray into the air.

The hardboiled backfist cracks into Jimmie's jaw like a firecracker. A bloody, copper taste numbs his tongue. The sonofabitch sucker punched him! His friends and street-traffic-bystanders swarm around them. They hoot and holler and yell shit like: "Get him!", and: "Teach him a lesson!" It'd be shameful not to oblige.

He pounces forward with a punch. The punk barely dodges out of the way. His second punch lands. Knuckles squelch deep into soft eye-socket-flesh.

Lucas tumbles sideways, backwards. He catches himself before his face collides with the sidewalk. Blood spews to the pavement; his brow must be cut open. Before he can push himself up, his ribs erupt like a gunshot as the brute drives a kick into his side. Air shoves out of his lungs.

Jimmie smiles as the steel-toe of his boot connects. The

plummie slams faceup into the ground; cradles his side and gags for air. Blood gurgles up out of a gash above the boy's eye.

The crowd around them is loud. Friends chant his name.

"Jim-mie! Jim-mie!"

He spits a mouthful of blood out onto the graper's shirt. "Stay down, bitch." He turns to his pals with a grin and shrugs. The crowd gets louder.

"Jim-mie! Jim-mie!"

Lucas squirms, trying to catch his breath. Blood pools around his swollen left eye. Pours down the side of his face. Puddles in his ear. Spills out onto the sidewalk.

The brute struts around and flexes his muscles. The crowd is chanting; an orange mosh pit circle with their fishbone eyebrows, toaster oven abdomens, and wiffle ball antlers.

"Jim-mie! Jim-mie!"

Lucas thinks of his son, his unspoiled little boy, who deserves a better world that this; deserves a father that stands up to its injustices. Air floods back into his lungs. He forces himself to his feet and lunges at the prick.

Adrenaline is gasoline in Lucas's bloodstream.

Jimmie's friends yell "watch out!", so he glances towards the punk just in time to see a purple fist crash into his nose. Blood and snot spatters. Eyes water and sight blurs.

Lucas swings a series of fluid jabs and roundhouses: pistons firing in a diesel engine. Punches crack into the bastard's face. A cheekbone snaps. The cocky smile replaced with a look of pain, shock. Disgrace.

Jimmie's face and nose bleed, throb. A kick to his knee topples him down to the sidewalk. Pavement chews chunks of skin off his elbow and forearm. The palm of his hand.

The chanting fades.

His face is a bonfire. His cheek feels hollow, caved-in.

The brittle shell of his lobster-tail chin cracked open. What the hell just happened?

"It's over," the plummie says.

Jimmie nods his head. Confused, dizzy.

Lucas sheds a nod of relief, fists loosen. He turns back up the street, careful of his smashed ribcage.

Rage seeps from Jimmie's marrow. Humiliation burns hotter than his battered face. He jolts himself upright, grabbing a beer bottle off the table. He charges the punk with a growl and clanks him in the back of the head.

Lucas's vision flashes lightning-white then blots out. He crumples to the ground.

Jimmie rolls him onto his back and climbs on top of him, dropping righthanded fists. The sound of their impact changes from hard smacks to sloppy splats as the purple's face goes mushy and he's breathing blood.

"Take THAT, you goddam graper! Put your filthy hands on me…"

Blood splatters all over the sidewalk. All over Jimmie. Anger drowns his friends' pleas to stop before he murders again.

Someone yells, "you racist motherfucker!" The crowd shrieks, scrambles. He looks up, sees an orange man with a faucet sprouting out of his forehead who's pointing a handgun at him. A revolver that pukes fire and lead, the explosive blow heaving Jimmie's body out into the street.

Lucas's lifeless body bleeds into the gutter, meeting the gore of a bullet ripping through Jimmie's lobster-tail chin and throat. Their blood blends together, both bodies feeding the same crimson puddle in the street.

Home Sick

something like…
the captive housefly
hanging--coiled--from our ceiling
to wither/starve/thirsting
for an easy way to die.
what about…tired
tubes of toothpaste:
malnourished, innards
barrowed/forgotten/taken
(purged of purpose).
or…the cigarette ashes
straying in the breeze out front,
homeless leftovers/remains
of former comfort.
maybe…the litter box:
black nests of fresh ammonia
(stinging nostrils)
neglected/ignored/unseen
shit clumping within.
…like your handgun
(revolver) locked away
from dust and bullets,
alone/vacant/without
its Man-given sex appeal.

: because when you're gone
this place isn't home
for me either.

Sun Kissed

The man managed to find (logistically speaking) the worst possible location in the mud pit; too far from the center to gather any real moisture for rehydration, yet also too far from the edge to avoid getting stuck. I say 'man' because whatever it was, it appeared to be male...but I'm not an expert on these things. Mans are intriguing creatures anyway. Historians said they use to be bigshots once, which added to my curiosity. This one, imprisoned in muck and roasting in the sun, happened to be the first I could observe up close.

Resting in the sand just beyond the edges of the mud pit, shading beneath a mature sage and congratulating myself on the decision to divorce Eleanor, I watched the man, sun-bleached and wobbly, come out of the desert seeking water and get lodged in the mud. As a younger lizard I would've gotten closer and poked it with a stick, but at my age I found the whole ordeal to be simply fascinating.

I'd been having dreams where I tried to scurry for shade only to find the sand too slick, too deep, and no matter how fast I scuttled I could barely move. Almost as if my thin, green tail weighed as much as a rattlesnake. I presumed the muddy mammal knew exactly how that felt—it would've loved to dash around at that particular moment if it could.

Eventually, the man realized that struggling was useless. Its head, with hair the color of beetles; a prickly, bearded face; and an upper limb were the only body parts not suffocating in mud. Its dumb, feral eyes peered out into the desert, darting between the chaotic shapes of layered rock which ranged in color from pale, seasick green to day-old-sunburn (as if a giant once spread multicolored spackle across the desert and left it to dry like a sporadically textured ceiling). Looking into its cactus-green eyes, I suspected it knew that it was dying. Surely mans understood the concept of death—instinctively rather than intellectually, of course.

As the sun slithered across the sky, I watched as the primate's hairless flesh shrunk and cracked into a thousand peeling pieces.

The man evaporated until it earned the trust of the thirsty dirt, ironically just out its reach.

Studying the creature led to pondering my dreams. Why couldn't I scamper? What was weighing me down? Given that morning's events back home, surely the dreams were my subconscious telling me that marriage held me back from experiencing life.

I imagined the man was capable of complex thought and contemplated the landscape's origin as it died. It wondered if the mountains were all once massive cubes of rock, melting in the desert sun over thousands of years to form the cliffs and arches.

Its throat and tongue were sandstone. They had to be in that heat.

Plump blisters the color of wood ticks peppered the mammal's skin. I licked the air and swabbed the roof of my mouth for a whiff of smoldering flesh, which kind of reminded me of Eleanor's cockroach casserole.

After a while, its eyes slowed and relaxed, accepting the fact that it wouldn't survive. It stared at a dead, shriveled sage brush not far from where I lay as if preparing itself for decay; the bush's gray withered branches reaching out like tendrils infected with flakes of brittle orange lichen; twisted, fractured metal speckled with rust.

It'd still moan and wiggle a bit on occasion, as if struggling to decide what posture it wanted to become fossilized in. Maybe it thought this to be important, like some kind of final unity with the dust that birthed it?

As the sky changed to milkweed for the setting sun, the primate stopped resisting the mud's tight embrace altogether. Its breathing became obviously more painful. It made some raspy choking noises and a weak whimper before its squinty eyes closed to unconsciousness.

Once it finally perished, I knew I just witnessed something beautiful and, quite literally, very dirty. In turn, I *felt* both beautiful and dirty…even my eyes seemed filthy from watching the man's pre-death cremation.

I tongued my ocular turrets, slurping them clean, and began to dig my burrow beneath the familiar sage.

Silly Love Poem

Poets write love
as marshmallow hot chocolate
in cottontail snow.
No(!)
Love is the sun and moon,
sharing equal watch over the sky
and keeping the tides accountable
for their actions.

Secondhand

T*hey scheduled the visitation on a Tuesday morning, closed casket of course, with the graveside service shortly after, followed by luncheon at the church. He would've found the whole ceremony pretentious, but Mother insisted.*

That summer Brother picked me up on Saturday mornings, triggering restless Friday nights, although hearing the backfire of his rust-colored Ford pickup coming down the street slew any sleepiness. He'd ignore Mother's gaze as I climbed in, often driving away before my seatbelt was buckled, like an escape pod in those space opera TV shows, ejecting from the mothership of weekday bore.

He and Mother hadn't been family since Father died.

Inside the truck, split navy-blue vinyl upholstery smelled like cigarettes and fast food, an odor Brother referred to as *unkillable*. A plastic case full of ashtray runaways and worn cassette tapes, some glued together with spattered soda, sat in the middle of the torn bench seat between us.

"Pick a tape," he said. "That collection is a soundtrack from the long dead cocaine days of rock and roll."

I always felt like an adult when he talked to me like that. He even let me watch rated-R movies, mostly action and slasher flicks, so long as I didn't tell Mother.

Fingering through the tapes, I asked, "Did you know Dave Mustaine from Megadeth was one of the original members of Metallica?" Or, "Iggy Pop's first high school band was called The Iguanas. That's where he got his name."

He said something about "always wanting to have a rock and roll documentary riding shotgun," a smile betraying his sarcasm.

Sometimes he took me into town to the basketball courts, or to an afternoon matinee. We even went swimming down at the YMCA from time to time. But we usually just hung out at his place in the country, a leaky singlewide he bought from a friend, the yellowing vinyl siding cracked and peeling.

His girlfriend, Sarah, made me toast with cinnamon and sugar when she wasn't working double shifts at the diner.

Most visits he tinkered with his Ford while the radio played in the background, hood propped up, skin stained with the smell of engine oil and antifreeze. I watched while throwing a ball for their dog, a heeler named Fray. Sometimes, he even taught me a few things about auto mechanics, letting me help by fetching things for him.

Sockets and wrenches.

Greasy, worn-out hand tools.

Lukewarm beer from the fridge inside.

I often asked about souped-up engines and turbo chargers. His truck could be *fast* like in the movies. He'd tease and tell me the clunker would fall apart if it went any faster. Still, I always asked because he'd let me help more when I did.

Movies and TV taught me everything about funerals. Rosaries and 21-gun salutes. Black Victorian riding hats with netted veils. Widows in dark lace gloves sucking smoke from long cigarillo holders like exhaust pipes.

One time he brought Fray with him to pick me up, a hot day in mid-July when even the breeze felt faded and warm. We stopped at the park before leaving town to linger on the manicured wild grass lawn, Brother lounging on his back beneath a shade tree, smoking a cigarette while I watched Fray chase squirrels.

A girl jogged by on the sidewalk, blood-blonde hair pulled back and tucked beneath her Walkman's headphones. Arctic-blue spandex jogging suit with matching tennis shoes. She was older than me, maybe a high-schooler.

He said something like "pretty girl", which startled me. I didn't answer, instead looking away, pretending to watch anything else. Cottontail clouds, Fray wrestling with a big stick, growling and huffing while wagging his tail.

He asked if there were any girls that I liked.

"*Like,* like?" I asked.

"Yes *like,* like," he replied, a lazy smirk on his face.

"Nah. Girls at school just like the older boys. And I look young for my age"

"I think you look your age. Maybe a little older."

He sat up, brushing his cigarette out against the elm tree's craggy gray bark, and said, "The problem is that you grew up watching twenty-somethings playing teenagers on TV, so of course you think you look young."

"So, what? Girls are *weird* anyway."

He laughed and said my feelings would change. That soon girls would be the *only* thing I cared about. I'd fall in love and have a whole new reason to be alive.

"Like you and Sarah?" I asked, tossing a vagrant pinecone for Fray to fetch.

"Right." After a moment he asked, "How would you feel if me and Sarah got married?"

"So, she'd be kind of like my big sister?"

"Yep, that's what they mean when they say *sister-in-law.*"

"That'd be awesome! I bet mom has always wanted a daughter—"

"Mom doesn't know," he said, voice razor-blade sharp. "We don't exactly see eye-to-eye these days."

"I know, but why not?"

He lit another cigarette, exhaling a heavy lungful of smoke as he started to answer. "Look, I guess you're old enough to know this. Mom cheated on Dad before leaving him," he spoke slowly, pausing to take another drag, "so he killed himself. I'm sorry to have to be the one to tell you."

"I've known."

"Oh. I just assumed—"

"Father told me."

The gun was a .357 Magnum, 5-round revolver with a 2-1/4 inch barrel. They say he bought it at a pawn shop earlier that week. The bullet, a .38 Special, 125-grain jacketed hollow-point. Standard ammunition you can pick up at Walmart.

Brother was supposed to come get me every weekend that summer but skipped some in August after he ran Fray over with his truck. I spent those Saturday mornings sitting on the curb talking with Father, fading with every loud muffler.

Hindsight understands Mother's hideous reaction.

When we did get together, he would slump on the hand-me-down couch, or at the cardboard kitchen table, drinking beer and smoking stale cigarette butts, smelling increasingly wilted. He didn't make toast like Sarah did, let alone sugarcoat it for me. His place felt heavier and smaller without her frilly decor. Flowery paintings and ceramic doodads replaced with empty walls and blank shelves, smelling like he never cracked a window.

Sometimes he sat on the front porch, overflowing with

garbage bags full of empty beer cans. So far out in the country we'd hear cars coming for miles away. His shoulders perked as if every oncoming vehicle carried a special delivery, just for him. But they never stopped, so instead he'd watch them drive by without expression, shoulders drooping, drinking from liquor bottles that smelled like charcoal and seared leather.

One night I walked in on him in the bathroom. He sat on the sticky linoleum floor, bottle nearby, eyes soggy and blistered. "It wasn't your fault," I said, "everyone knows that all dogs go to heaven."

"Heaven? What are you talking about, *heaven*? I'll be out in a minute," he barked, slamming the door as I slunk away to whimper. Our favorite professional wrestling show started at nine-o'clock, the one we usually watched together, but I couldn't get reception on channel seven. Instead, I kneaded Father's lavender handkerchief between my thumb and forefinger, a commonplace habit with the ever-pocketed remnant.

What TV doesn't tell you is how strong the jolt of a snub-nose revolver's recoil is. The jaw shatters when one is fired inside someone's mouth. It's useless to search for every shard of tooth.

That last weekend we hung out together, Brother didn't say much when he picked me up. His shirt, orange like saltwater taffy, looked stained and wrinkled—more so than usual. His breath smelled like mouthwash, his sweat like liquor. He took the long way to his place, zigzagging along various backroads as if trying to avoid being tailed, like in those detective shows.

He slept all afternoon while I meandered through a static whiteout looking for something to watch on TV. When he finally woke he needed help finding the phone, so he could call Sarah. Their conversation was shorter than most television commercials, ending with him crumpling the phone and screaming, "*FUCK!*" teeth grinding behind his taut jaw. He didn't say anything for the rest of the night, instead sitting alone drowning cigarette butts in left-for-empty beer cans, some crushed like siblings.

At least he found channel seven in time for nine-o'clock wrestling.

Another thing TV doesn't tell you about is the sunburn when a fresh corpse rests outside for hours on a mid-September afternoon. The morticians draining body-length blisters. Summer sun on the pavement—imagine a peach on asphalt that steals your shoeprint.

Weeks passed before I went to go see Brother on my own. Mother would've been angry, so I didn't tell her before leaving early that morning. I walked until late afternoon, calling out for him once I got to his place. There was no answer, yet the front door was unlocked.

I found him on the back patio, face hollow, the back of his head sprinkled all over the pavement like divots on a golf course, a gun in his hands. The air tasted sour and putrid, but otherwise calm, birds twittering peacefully in the distance. The blood didn't bother me like it would most people in my grade—I'd seen enough scary movies to know all about gore.

Before calling 9-1-1, I pocketed a piece of his skull,

soggy with flesh and scalp, brains and blood, smuggling it home after the commotion of ambulances and police officers.

I hid him in an old fishbowl beneath my bed where Mother wouldn't find him, where he'd stay dark and moist. Where he could mold over. To this day his skull-fungus quivers when I take him out to feed him frogs or mice, maybe the occasional cockroach.

We still sit together and watch nine-o'clock wrestling every Saturday night, our Father, interwoven into his handkerchief—the torn corner of the sheet he used to hang himself—sprawled between us on the couch.

Profixer®

A re you generally dissatisfied with your life? Those everyday stresses of the middleclass American Dream got you down? Feeling too goddamn <u>human</u>? Fear not! We've got the solution for you—just *Swallow the Rainbow*™. Talk to your healthcare professional to see if the Profixer® Power Pack regimen is right for you.

Strawberry Monday:

• Taking two Red capsules with a glass of milk results in a state of butterfly bliss and twittery sunshine. Unicorns giving birth to rainbows in your cranial juices. Everything smells like ignorance and teddy bear dreams.

• *Side effects may include:* the bitter, quivering squeam of anxiety. A gut punch of bloodshot jitter. What if you're never the same again? What if *this* is the new normal? Whatif? Whatifwhatifwhatifwhatifwhatif?

Tangerine Tuesday:

• Taking an Orange pill on an empty stomach calms the tidal chaos of anxious breath. Your thought patterns coagulate, and your viscera engage in their standard post-riot activities.

• *Side effects may include:* bleak, dying, withering depression. A regulated maiming by the heavy windchimes of death. Gloom blankets your world, spoiling everything jovial and jolly. You're gonna drown in this. Gonna drown in this.

Lemon Wednesday:

• Dissolve a Yellow tablet in Taiwanese oolong tea and

sip over breakfast to exile the downcast demons back into the deep intestinal caverns where they dwell.

• *Side effects may include:* fistfuls of rage percolating alongside your spinal fluid. Blood grows ballistic with creeping, seeping, gurgling wrath. You need to destroy something…something beautiful.

Kiwifruit Thursday:

• A handful of Green pills before your morning piss shrinks the rage back down into manageable, random doses of annoyance.

• *Side effects may include:* vigorous, blistering heartburn. Digestive juices and corrosive enzymes hack away at esophagus tissues. Everything tastes like broiled flesh and campfire smoke. Drinking liquids only makes it worse.

Blueberry Friday:

• Taking a Blue pill (with a fiber-heavy snack) twice before lunch douses the acidic bonfire smoldering in your sternum.

• *Side effects may include:* an onslaught of cankerous mouth ulcers erupting blood and pus and anguish. Every pore of your tongue and cheeks prefer chewing on graveled glass over this torture. To salivate is to suffer.

Plum Saturday:

• Three Indigo gel capsules shrink mouth sores back into an acceptable state of dormancy, reducing pain from agony to measly irritant.

• *Side effects may include:* throbbing, thrashing cluster

headaches. The sinuses swell, blotting against your vision. Noises whisper-volume and up crack like car crashes inside your skull. A kitten's purr is a thunderous pistol whip.

Eggplant Sunday:

• Pop a Violet pill with your eucharist. The headaches dissolve. Sinuses melt and numb until pacified.

• *Side effects may include:* feelings of generic dissatisfaction with your pathetic, bullshit middleclass life. You're just too fucken human for this shit. But we've got pills for that!

Kitters

(-A-)
claiming a sun spot
on the carpet, grooming
her long hair like
a calico barn owl
licking its feathers
before a midnight feast

(-B-)
feverish with flea bite
hollow stomach and matted fur
blending in with the feral

blood in your feline hair
from bathing with
infected gums

anxiety and ungrace
has your cuddle and purr
fallen to the illness
old friend?

now you just yowl
at the door
hoping to sleep
in the sun

glocksucker

I haven't had an orgasm since puberty, an ejaculation that nearly killed me. I've been careful ever since, and going to the bar with Erica isn't smart. But when she discovers my little secret and asks me out for a drink, the tattoos of featureless red birds spiraling up her arms and out into the uncaged atmosphere, I can't decline.

Erica has tanglewood eyes and more ear piercings than I can count without sweeping her chestnut hair out of the way. Her lowcut shirt shows skin beneath her belly button and clings tight to her breasts, which are harnessed in a bra that jostles them about every time she moves. Blue jeans grip her ass like greedy hands.

The bar she chooses, a shithole named Shotgunners, is humid and spongy, with empty shot glasses scattered everywhere like spent shells on a battlefield. The crowd around the bar looms a dozen people thick, so a hundred-dollar bill ensures the bombshell waitress keeps our glasses full while we stake claim to the only vacant table (wet and sticky from spilt drinks).

We drink while bobbing-and-weaving through small talk. She licks her lips and watches my mouth move when I say things. Laughs at all my jokes, places her hand on my forearm when doing so.

"You really named your dick 'the Alamo'?" She asks, lighting a fresh cigarette before putting the old one out, its bittermint menthol smell swallowing both of us. She takes her smoke like a deep kiss.

"Yep, because you'll always remember it, hehe." Even I can't believe the dangerous, drunken pick-up lines I'm weaving.

"Oh, I'm *sure*," she mocks.

We drink more. She says her roommate is named Kiko

Magellan, which is bullshit—no one is named Kiko Magellan.

At some point an urban beat bounces through the speakers, decelerating life's natural vibrations. Everyone moves in slow motion, the skin on their faces slinking towards the ground like molten cheese. I hold my breath and count the stars inside my eyelids until the world resumes its average pace.

"Oh—I *love* this song. Wanna dance?" Erica asks, flushing the rest of her bloody mary down her throat. Without waiting for an answer, she floats out of her chair and moves towards a herd of dancers. I follow her onto a hardwood dancefloor that's scarred from high heel warfare.

She reaches back and interlocks her fingers behind my neck, shoulder blades against my chest. She strokes my earlobe, bites her lip, touches her face. My fingers slip across her stomach, smooth like top shelf scotch.

She arches her back, pressing her ass into my crotch.

Rolling thrusts against my dick.

Grinding. Twisting.

Her skin reminds me of honey. Her hair is all beachy waves and caramel highlights and giddy pheromones. I breathe it in.

My blood-enflamed penis makes its presence known. I think of naked George Washington with a mouthful of miniature politicians squirming between his teeth; wigless and hogtied to a stick, spit-roasting inside a microwave oven. Orgasmic fluids slow and coagulate, bulging and backlogging at the tip of my dick—a fire hose at the pinch point in an old timey cartoon.

"I'm not sure about this," I warn, but Erica either can't hear me or doesn't care. She rubs her hand against my erection inside my khakis. She bites her lower lip and looks achingly into my eyes. I kiss her, and she bites *my* lower lip when I try to pull away.

Her apartment is within drunken stumbling distance of the bar.

Sloppy, feral sex. She squeals as I thrust in and out, taking handfuls of her ass and spreading the cheeks apart to get just a little deeper. She arches her back to get herself as far up and out there as possible. Balls slap against her clit as she drips with syrupy satisfaction. I cram my unwashed thumb into her butthole, its acceptance tight and suctioning.

She gasps something about it being "so, so dirty".

Everything smells like cadmium and other heavy metals.

She slips a vibrator up her ass, alongside my thumb as I plunge away at her from behind. I watch in the mirror as her dangling breasts sway and jolt in every direction—tidal waves that grow from butt-cheek-ripples created by my jackhammering pelvis.

I jerk her head back by a fistful of her hair. Spank her ass until it welts. Squeeze her tit as hard as I can. Choke her from behind. Call her a slut. She screams for me to fuck her. Harder.

The pressure. Builds. Then erupts. In blood, and cum.

And bullets.

9mm slugs spray everywhere like killer rain, ripping open the end of my penis in a pleasureful, painful, pitiful sensation. Tearing through her uterus, lungs, throat, and detonating out the top of her head, leaving a mushy stump where her scalp used to be. Hot shell casings burn flesh as they splay out of me and ricochet off the wall, the mattress, Kiko Magellan's exposed erection in the corner chair. Bullets, smoke, the smell of gunpowder.

Relief, sweet euphoric relief.

Her body crumples to the bed, tanglewood eyes still open.

Blood and dead bird tattoos and cum and bullet-holes and shell casings everywhere.

———

"There's no way you're a virgin…virgins don't fuck that good," Erica says, lying jumbled in her sheets without any fucking left in her, sharing a minty cigarette with Kiko. Her words suck me back into the current dimension, the one without blood and black powder residue.

My slut slayer did its job, like always. It's time to go writhe in guilt and grief and regret until the urge to hunt again becomes unbearable. I get dressed and leave without saying a word.

Second Coming

(For: Jessi)

and I feel
that I'm finding
my world's been shaken.

By a nutmeg blonde;
that static pulse
in her blue-jean eyes.

900 days and still
electric bombshells
burst in my belly:

butterfly shrapnel.

A passionate rebirth of
this—the purest pulp
of human emotion

boiling over.

Aftertaste

"**Y**ou've got a father, sure," she says. "But you'll always be a bastard to me."

Door slams; she's gone. Forever this time.

Tomorrow her things will be thrown into boxes and piled in the backseat of her car. Empty drawers and windows without curtains. Shampoos, light bulbs, triple-A batteries. Anything that was even *maybe* hers: packed up and hauled off.

In exchange for her house key.

An inevitable conclusion, in hindsight. When you begin a relationship in rehab the outcome can't be good. At least you started with common interests.

Her love's unhealthy and you can tell from the start. But you're convinced you can stay one step ahead of her--you've seen these games before. Until you become fond of her sexy little half-smile and sandalwood scent. Her bonfire sex. Hacking away at your defenses with a hammer and chisel.

Flaking off in little shards like hard candy.

Much like a druggie whittling the electrical contact out of a light bulb. Homemade paraphernalia.

And then it's too late. Just hearing her name tingles like a rollercoaster's plunge. Your hasty heartbeat feeds a twitterpated bloodstream. You buy her a silver ring and offer sloppy promises.

Regardless of what your heart says, in the end, it was always about the sex.

Soon that bright, warm, electric feeling fades. As if someone reached in with a rusty pair of needle-nose pliers and ripped out the lighting filament. Being together becomes habit. When she's not around you feel like you can hardly breathe.

You drive around town, looking for her. Knock on her sister's door. Her parent's. Her ex-husband's.

You do whatever it takes just for a taste. But you're ashamed the moment your craving's quenched.

Of course, at this point she's spending more time at the bar than home. Evenings together become loud disputes. Apologies. She bloodies your nose. You break the bathroom window. Makeup sex.

Ravage. Resolve. Repeat.

Until all that's left is an empty glass shell.

Like the bulb you use to smoke your powders.

Your methamphetamines. Your cocaine. Crushed painkillers.

Eventually, the heat cracks split and the whole thing falls apart in your hands.

A one-time friend of yours comes to her rescue, saving the goddamn day.

You've found silver rings go for $10 at Browse-n-Pawn. At least, that's what she tells you.

A slamming door echoes around your last rational thoughts.

The peak before the come-down.

Scar tissue for tomorrow.

Spare Change

churchy community Christmas tree
hinting gift ideas for needy families
the ones that just want
tents that don't leak
and blankets w/out holes
to keep their families out of the
Chattahoochee seasons.
the ones that secretly wish for
a new pair of shoes (men's size 10).
the ones sleeping on asphalt.

but i've thrown Change at
Salvation Army coffers
so i curl on the couch
with my cat—frost collecting on
car windows outside.

Snow Globe

W inter mornings like this are the deadliest.

The clouds press against the terrain, casting flat, gray light. Big, fuzzy snowflakes meander towards the ground. The atmosphere is still and quiet as the crystalized air absorbs both breeze and sound. It seems warm, too warm to be winter; chilly on your nose and cheeks, but not *freezing* like you would expect. Trees are decorated in deep frost; some look like frozen fishbone ribcages. Others, hunkered under the weight, look like crippled hands, the skin drizzling from the bone in hoary waves of frozen froth. Scattered pine trees are like drunken gray-green triangle smears in the fog.

"Is this a dream?" your brain asks. And that's exactly what Winter wants you to think. "This serene, calm tundra is harmless," it says. Yet it will not hesitate to take your toes through frostbite, nor freeze your lips to chop-sicles.

Winter mornings like this can be deadlier than the blizzardy yowl or the icy wasteland…at least *then* you somewhat expect to die.

Punching holes through the knee-deep snow, you track prey that doesn't leave tracks. If not for the pink trail of blood blots scattered every so often, there would be no tracking to be had.

These woods are tranquil and peaceful, part of Winter's trap. Visibility is low due to fog and snowfall. It's easy to lose track of time. You could be wandering around out here for hours before realizing you're lost, freezing, dying.

The blood stains in the snow are spaced just far enough to keep you on path towards your wounded prey.

Winter takes more than a few souls each year, out here in these very woods. You can't see the sun, nor the mountains. It may not be coming down hard, but the snow is falling thicker than you realize and even your own tracks are quickly filled in with fresh powder. Which way is town again?

Each pink blemish of blood is a beacon directing your way.

Even the squeaky crunch of your own footsteps is muffled and distorted in the winter air: every noise is faint and fuzzy. It's details like this that fool your brain into thinking you're dreaming. We all know that you can't freeze to death in a dream.

The only way to survive is to focus on the task at hand, the slow and steady pace of trudging through the snow. Focus on the kill, the harvest. It's too easy to get taken away with the majestic beauty of these woods, and in a wonderland such as this, one step staggered in the wrong direction will surely lead to getting lost, getting frozen, getting dead.

It's that real. It's that dangerous.

You see the copper-colored blob in the foggy distance before you hear it, but the sizzling of snowflakes on hot metal wafts in soon after, hissing and spitting like bacon grease in a cast iron skillet. With each step it fades more into view, and you recognize it to be a rocket-powered jetpack, still hot from use, melting the snow it rests in. It's bumped and bruised from a rough landing and will eventually rust to death before anyone else finds it.

Never mind that—where is the operator?! Were they hurt in the crash? The only thing worse than being lost in these wintery woods is being lost *and* injured. Something else leaks in from the fog as you gain ground on the jet pack. Not far from the crash site, you see a young girl lying among the cherry slush of bloody snow.

God, no! Are you too late?

You sprint towards her, the weight and suction of the frozen powder weighing down your stride. Hot breath evaporates from her nostrils. She's alive!

She squirms, weak and whimpering, sounds that disappear behind you as they're soaked up into the air's black hole void of silence. All she's wearing are blood-soaked pajamas—no jacket or coat—and her garlic blonde hair is already frozen. Her bruise-colored eyes barely flicker as you kneel beside her.

"Ssssshhhhhhhh."

You pinch her mouth closed to damper the cry as you jerk the huntsman's blade out of her femur where you left it as she rocketed away towards the woods. You wipe the frost from the polyurethane tusks sprouting from her jowls and reach for the hacksaw hanging from your belt. Even on a morning like this, you'd do best to work fast as a search party can't be far behind.

Cold Front

This time of year
always depresses me.

Halter-tops and miniskirts
are tucked away in the backs of closets,
next to tacky Christmas sweaters.

Windowsills become housefly
graveyards, the only survivors
fat and pathetic in their bumbling flight.

All the songbirds are sipping
mojitos on some beach in Mexico.

Autumn's artwork of leaves now
litter the gutter like little
yellow skeletons.

I think people were intended
to hibernate. Even the days are tired,
going to bed earlier and earlier.

Mess

Don't worry, she said, it's just a mess.

Heartsickening. The condom on my cock split like a chapped lip.

Blame *any*thing but me. Sure, her vagina felt unfamiliar. Parched—not dry like sandpaper. Think cottonmouth. Maybe *that's* my fault, but still.

Don't worry, it's just a mess.

Faulty contraceptive. One of those colored types for aesthetic pleasure. Or aesthetic horror: red latex wrapped around the base of your dick. A penis in candy-apple panties.

Fast-forward:

A thick glob of red/brown tissue. Blood clots and mucous--human yolk. Scum water and toilet bowl cleaner. Scooped up in a pickle jar and crammed into the fridge.

Behind the liquid egg whites.

Just a mess.

Psychosomatical

T odd escaped in his morning showers. The spray of sweltering water. The rhythm and bruise of mist spewing from the nozzle against his skin. His coping mechanisms for life's stresses. Asshole bosses, probation officers, delinquent payments, custody battles; none of it mattered when in the sanctuary behind that moldy shower curtain.

His shower that morning was no different.

At first.

Water blasted against the unshaved stubble of his scalp and face, pouring down his body, when something brushed his foot. He opened his eyes and watched a pencil shaving, a corrugated half-spiral flake of graphite-tipped clay, wash out around his foot, flow downstream, and get pinned against the drain by the water escaping into the pipes below.

"The hell?!" he thought aloud, looking behind him to the back of the tub to find it just as clueless as to how a pencil shaving got into the shower with him. Two more pencil shavings floated down from above into the trickle at his feet. He inspected the popcorn plastered ceiling. Nothing but a couple of rust colored mildew colonies.

This curious event brought with it the anxieties of Todd's life: public transit, antiviral genital ointment, dodging the landlord. The sanctuary of the shower was corrupted, now a hideous and vile thing.

Todd turned the water off, stepped out of the shower, and wrapped a bath towel around his waist. Despite the exhaust fan in the bathroom ceiling, steam and humidity rolled out as he opened the door and stepped out into the hallway.

A low, mechanical hum vibrated throughout the house.

Todd recognized the noise from somewhere, but couldn't place it. Not the bathroom's exhaust fan. He walked through the living room and cracked open the blinds to peer outside, looking for evidence of a street truck or a douchebag neighbor with some new project. Anything that could be responsible for the groaning sound. Nothing.

Todd crouched down and reached up under the lip of his secondhand coffee table, grabbing the butterfly knife he kept hidden there.

Flick-twist, the butterfly blade brandished.

Knife eager, Todd followed the noise into the kitchen and flung open a few empty cupboard doors, half expecting to find a boisterous orgy of Number 2 pencils. Nothing.

Inside the oven, the room temperature refrigerator. Nothing.

He paused to consider the empty rubber cement jar and crumpled, brown paper lunch sack on the table, reassuring himself that the humming was real. The pencil shavings in the shower were real. They *were* real, dammit!

The raspy whine continued its endless grind.

Todd made his way down the hall into his bedroom. Everything was as he remembered, the bed unmade, shoes and clothes and clutter scattered everywhere. Mr. Truffles, his half blind Siamese cat, sat in the window sill staring up at the air vent in the ceiling, a fierce flick to his tail.

The ceiling vents. Of course!

He hurried back up the hall and into the kitchen, yanking open the junk drawer. Digging through mismatched batteries, assorted paperclips, crusted and crumbling condoms. Clips and hinges and random shit he saved over the years. Where the hell was the screwdriver?

Back into the living room. Beneath the chair? No. Behind the old, boxy TV? No. Couch cushions tossed aside but still no goddam screwdriver.

Fuck it, the butterfly blade would work. He rushed back

into the kitchen where he left the blade on the counter. A heap of pencil peelings slipped out of a ceiling vent and twisted to the living room floor below.

The raspy whine continued its endless grind.

Back in his room with the knife, Todd climbed atop his mattress where he could just reach the vent cover. He fit the tip of the blade into the screwhead's slot and twisted, working the fastener out of place where it fell into a nest of shavings on the floor.

Next screw, same routine; but the blade slipped from the slot on slashed into the tip of his index finger. Ow, fuck! It was a bleeder.

He hopped down off the mattress, leaving the vent cover hanging cockeyed on one screw, and ran towards the bathroom to flush the gash with cold water. He stopped at the bathroom door where he found the floor covered knee-deep in pencil flakes. More shavings toppled down out of the exhaust fan's vent as the pile grew and started seeping out of the door into the hallway.

Still high on the primeval shock of a deep cut, Todd backed into the kitchen. Forgetting about the wound, blood wept from his fingertip, blotting everything he touched a crimson red.

A waist-high mound of pencil shavings loitered on the kitchen floor. It grew as he watched more pour out of the ceiling vent, quickly spreading out to bury the rest of the linoleum.

A cedary, wood-clinched scent blitzed his nostrils.

Todd glanced over to see the living room also overflowing with shavings. He thought about running for the front door, but a loud clank from the bedroom shattered his concentration. The vent cover must've fallen.

He stood frozen and confused, scared. It wasn't real. No way it could be real. Right?

The raspy whine continued its endless grind, like a headache that never fades.

A coarse yelp shrieked down the hall from his room. Mr. Truffles! Please God, no!

Fear shrunk back into its pothole as he hurried back to his bedroom. By then the hallway was up to his naval in shreds of pencil skin, quickly ripping the bath towel away from his body. He waded nude through the stingy, itchy, prickly shavings; stride heavy as if mucking through deep snow or mud that got stickier with each stride.

Finally into the bedroom! Todd could barely see Mr. Truffle's feline face, void pistachio eyes, mouth forced open and shoved full of shavings—lifeless. Tears rushed to Todd's eyes, but he'd have to mourn later; the pencil shavings were already to his armpits.

Swimming, clawing, tearing away at the pencil peels. Stabbing, slicing, biting into his skin; blood soaked shavings. If he could just make it to the window! Pace slowed. Shavings piled higher, blocking sunlight from outside. Trudging stopped as the pencil fodder crammed in too tight to move anymore.

Panic exploded in his head like a throttled can of beer. Rising shaving levels, past his shoulders, past his throat. He couldn't move a finger. Couldn't wiggle a toe.

Choking. Gagging. The taste of plastic-pipe-tap-water clogging his throat, blocking all airways. Stomach bloated, filling with shavings. This isn't real, isn't real! Please God, this isn't real!

Todd looked up into the coverless ceiling vent as more pencil shavings gushed out. He saw it. An old, wall-mount, schoolhouse pencil sharpener with bladed worm gears, just humming away and devouring pencils. Its handle spun fast, like an airplane propeller.

Shavings crept in and covered his face. It could've been his eyesight starting to collapse with the white lights of death. Or it could've been the pencil shavings stabbing into his eyes. But the last thing Todd saw was the pencil sharpener's face. Eyes beaming, vicious smile.

The raspy whine continued its endless grind.

Partake

A month before summer when cottonwood flakes float on nothing like paper ashes, the time of year when mother made her famous Caucasian Casserole with fried nipples and pancreatic sausage [doused in great-gamma's secret tonsil sauce]. Crockpot witchery. It's during this death rattle of springtime when I grind inside my husk, wearing corduroy flip-flops and drinking diet cocktails. Smoking fat-free cigarettes.

Backwards children frolic in the meadow below my nest, pointing, commenting on my laser white eyes. I crave slurping their slick ribs like sticky fingers.

Cracking open their knee joints to suckle upon like freshwater mollusks.

Dipping their toes in Worcestershire and swallowing whole.

Even now the children throw rocks, hoping to knock me from my perch to watch me tumble, watch me smear into the ground. Watch me lick the gravel from my wounds. Scrutinize me whilst I piss unto the tarmac clay, molding mud to pack against my ribcage swellings.

Fuck them and their youthful trickery. It's been so long since I chewed sinew, since I had the teeth for it.

Greedy tears overboil just from thinking on it. The liver [or whatever organ resists within] sore and sour and altogether messy.

Hey there, a boy calls, *what are you doing, always dormant and wrapped within yourself up there?*

I'm never-neverlanding—I reply—would you like a taste?

Just a bit, I suppose, he says, climbing unto my roost. *Is it true what they say? The stories of your treachery?*

Kind of, depending on what you've heard and of which you are asking.

Lullabies of a flesh eater, a bone picker, the Wyvern Lord of the Anthropophagi. A monster that marinates children's hearts in liver juices.

Marrow, actually. Marinated in marrow, the slippery syrup of greater eras. Alas, I am no longer this eater of children, devourer of folk. I am old, and I decompose within my den, fatigued and starving [my voice: crackly and crooked].

Never again to indulge in human meat? The boy soaks upon the pain of this stanch old man.

Outwardly I laugh and sigh and giggle and cry. Inside I am young, just without the strength to pander in cannibalistic choreography.

Please, the boy says, offering a wrist, *drink from my bloodstream.*

Quiet, young one—I say—you know not of what you are asking.

Really, you must. I am alone in this world and will surely perish before long. Let me offer myself as sacrifice to the Erstwhile Gods so that I can die for a cause.

Snap of the neck, sip of the spinal juices, filling the cleft within my digestive tract. Tempt me once…

Tastes like fillet-o-fish, his dermis spattered within my guts, bloating my pores. Contemporary children are all poisoned by the mar of modern convenience. Their meat is tainted, near spoiled, only angering hunger aches. This putrid feed is why my kind are going extinct—not for the laws of man. They've chosen starvation. Except I, the stubborn old fool inside a cockleshell of denial and decay.

Under-tolling my words, I whisper to the boy's carcass: the Erstwhile Gods are all dead.

Vanished, you say? he asks as I gnaw at his bladder sac, my tarter-sauce-scent of stagnate and bowel-rot weakening in stench. *Understanding your prose is an uneasy task.*

Without a trace—I respond in blech—ergo, they <u>must</u> be dead.

Exterminated, maybe? the boy asks from within my veins.

You could be right—I ponder, the boy's skeletals scattered about the base of my perch. Younger children below play with his collar bone, toss his skull to and fro. Sword fight with his femurs, still wet with salivate.

Zero gods answer the cries of present generations—I beclaim, picking tendon scrapings from my teeth—that's the only thing left to comfort unto anyone, boy.

Story Behind the Stories

In the years after learning that poetry is something much more than the crap I wrote in high school, *Outside Writer's Collective* published the following three poems in 2010 and 2011. "Cold Front" was my prize piece coming out of a poetry class at the College of Southern Idaho in 2009. Many poems in different forms eventually became "The Everyday", which is basically a gathering of thoughts and feelings collected as I struggled with life after drugs and alcohol (I've been sober since June 8, 2007). "Second Coming" is a love poem to my amazing wife before we were married, the best poem I've ever written and probably the only reason she married me. It also appeared in *Twelve Point Collective Volume 2: Modern Relationships* (2017).

Regarding prose, "Mess" is an exaggerated reflection of a circumstance from my late teens which ended up being my first piece of fiction to get published (*Pulp Fiction Magazine*, 2010). Years later, it also appeared alongside some of my other work in *The Drip Drop Prophet & Other Stories* (NihilismRevised, 2018).

I wrote "Aftertaste", published by the now defunct *Troubadour 21* (2011), as a throwback to whatever tangible skills I learned as a druggie. I wouldn't be the same person if not for those dark years of my life, and this piece of flash fiction remains one of my personal favorites when choosing from my own work.

Shortly after getting married, my wife and I moved to the South for several years as I pursued opportunities with my day job. My family would travel back west for several weeks each summer while I stayed for work. To keep from going crazy while they were gone, my mind drifted back into that of a poet, writing what would later be a collection of five poems published by *Soft Cartel* (2018): "Rousting", "Spare Change", "Silly Love Poem", "Home Sick", and "Kitters" (a poem about a cat of mine who became anemic with flea infestation and deteriorated into a feral insanity until veterinary medicine finally brought her back).

While living in the South, I also continued to rework "Secondhand", the earliest draft written back in 2008. I once considered this short story my greatest feat as a writer. I fancied it a deep and emotional work of literary fiction. It was eventually published by *Bartleby Snopes*, a magazine that, at the time, was accepting less than 7% of stories submitted to them (according to Duotrope statistics). They published it both online and in issue #10 of their print magazine (2013), a personal milestone that I will forever be grateful for. Recently rereading this piece, however, was a bit of a disappointment —not because *Snopes* was wrong about it by any means, but because my voice and personal style has changed so much since it was written. After some deliberation, I decided to rewrite "Secondhand" specifically for this collection, adding meat to its minimalist bones and using language that better reflects what my writing voice has developed into. I feel that this piece is now complete... a decade after I scribbled the first draft.

After a few years hiatus while focusing on family and career, "Recovery" is basically a true story laced with violent language regarding the viral symptoms of influenza. It was first published in *Long Day Press: Journal 2* (2017) and appeared in *The Drip Drop Prophet & Other Stories* (NihilismRevised, June 2018).

"Sun Kissed" was my first attempt at writing straight up weird fiction, specifically finding a mentor to help me write bizarro. It originally appeared at *Bizarro Central* (2017) and was also published in *The Drip Drop Prophet & Other Stories* (NihilismRevised, 2018).

I wrote my first piece of what I consider bizzaro horror in "Psychosomatical". I love this weird little story. This piece was originally printed in *Strange Behaviors: An Anthology of Absolute Luridity* (NihilismRevised, 2018).

"Snow Globe" is another brief piece of bizarro horror that originally appeared at *Bizarro Central* (2018). It also appeared in *The Drip Drop Prophet & Other Stories* (NihilismRevised, 2018). There have been rumors that a short film inspired by this story is in preliminary discussions. These rumors are true.

"Violet Crime or Secondary Colors" is definitely the most politically driven piece I've written to date, making a mockery of racism and violence. It was first published in *The Drip Drop Prophet & Other Stories* (NihilismRevised, 2018).

. . .

I worked on "Profixer" off and on since late 2007. It started as a poem then became short story. Then it was a poem again. It finally found its home in the flash fiction format published at *Silent Motorist Media* (2018).

Don't ask me what inspired "Glocksucker" because all I really know is that it's a despicable piece of scummy horror that isn't fit for human consumption. Unless you're the editors or fan base of *Horror Sleaze Trash*, as they published it a few months ago (2018) and I'm thankful to be a part of what they are doing.

"Partake" was fun to write because I chose to put constraints upon this piece to force creative juices to percolate in new ways. Each line starts with the next letter of the alphabet (save for "X", in which I allowed myself to use the "ex" sound instead). Most people don't notice until I tell them. Did you? Also note that this piece will be reprinted in *Where There Are Dragons: An Anthology of Mixed Emotions*, which is a mixed-genre charity anthology benefiting suicide prevention and mental health awareness coming February 2019 from Robber's Dog Pub.

"Innards" is an example of taking a big idea and chewing down into something small and absurd. It appears in *F*cked Up Stories to Read in the Daytime: Collected Stories to Damage Your Children*, a limited zine by Filthy Loot which will hit the streets around the same time this collection is published.

. . .

Earlier I mentioned administering constraints while writing a piece to force creativity to flow in new ways, a method I learned from Blake Butler in an online class (P.S. check out LitReactor's online writing classes—they're amazing!). "Benchwarmer" uses one of these constraints as, although a short piece, it is made up of one sentence. I got the idea from a couple authors that I admire who have written short stories using this technique, both much longer than this one. This book features the first printing of "Benchwarmer".

Austin James writes with caffeine in his blood, gypsy spit in his spinal fluid, and an incredibly lazy pseudonym. His prose and poetry have been published in multiple magazines and medias.